Dedicated to my niece, Lilia.

B&F
Brook & Field Publishing

Lilia and the Giant Bumblebee by Amanda Goodchild

Published by Brook and Field Publishing
www.brookandfieldpublishing.com

Illustrated by Finchenko Maria

Book cover and internal design by Gemma Mason www.thepeanut.co.uk

With special thanks to Sophia and Zoe Goodchild for their creative input and to Anya McKee for her assistance with editing the manuscript.

For permissions contact: info@brookandfieldpublishing.com

ISBN Print Edition 978-1-7397712-0-1

Printed in the United Kingdom.
First Edition printed 2022.

Lilia and the Giant Bumblebee

Amanda Goodchild

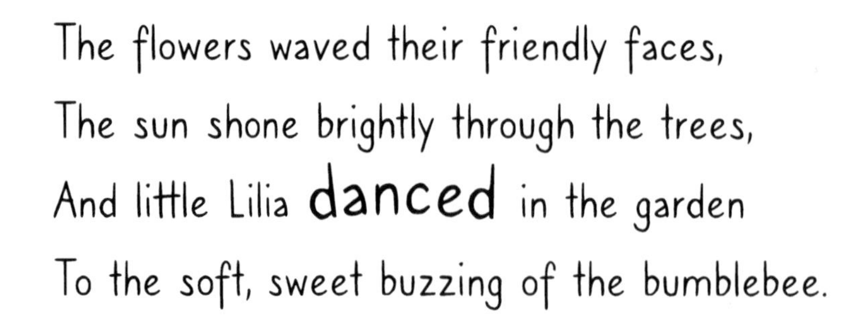

The flowers waved their friendly faces,
The sun shone brightly through the trees,
And little Lilia **danced** in the garden
To the soft, sweet buzzing of the bumblebee.

Buzz, the stripy bumblebee,
Was different from the rest.
He was the biggest of them all;
Sweet Lilia liked him best.

His wings flashed and shimmered,
They glistened with light,
As quickly he darted
Away, out of sight.

At the back of the garden, behind an old tree,
Little Lilia followed him fast.
She peered beneath the undergrowth,
Through the roots and mossy grass.

She heard his **buzz,** for it was loud,
But the bee she could not see,
'Til she noticed a little gleam of light
From right inside the tree!

The ray of light was a shimmery hue,
It looked like liquid gold.
Gazing in wonder, Lilia was curious,
Then it lit up some words and told ...

Of the Land of the Giant Bumblebees and the Kingdom of Butterflies.

Then Lilia carefully touched the words
And a hole opened up inside!

Lilia sat down at the foot of the tree
And stared at the cave within.
But the light was warm,
And it seemed to say,
'Little girl it is safe to come in.'

Then suddenly, from deep within the tree,
The giant bumblebee did appear!
He spoke in a quiet and gentle voice:

'We need you, child, do not fear.'

'Follow me,' Buzz said, and Lilia did,
She gently crawled inside.
The hole became a giant cave
Full of purple, radiant light.

Lilia looked around in wonder,
She was smaller than the bumblebee.
But her new friend, Buzz, just grinned and said,

'Jump up, you
can ride on me!'

The bee took off at lightning speed,
And Lilia held on tight.

They soared and swooped and twirled and looped,

Then gracefully ended their flight.

She found herself in an unknown place;
This world had a purple sky.
It was the Land of the Giant Bumblebees,
And the Kingdom of Butterflies!

They gently landed amidst a stone circle
With creatures all crowding around.
They all flapped their wings,
And the noise was immense
As Lilia stepped out onto the ground.

In front of her stood the king and his queen,
Her face had a worried look.
'Young Lilia,' she said, 'Will you help us, please,

Can you read us the words in this book?'

A servant came forward with an old leather book,
Resting gently in his hands.

'Our kingdom is slowly dying,' he said,

'Yet in these pages is **hope** for our land.'

The Queen continued in a solemn voice:
'We don't know what to do.
We cannot read, but we know that you can.
Please Lilia–your friends—we need you.'

Lilia smiled, she was happy to help,
Her mind was quick and clear.
She blew off the dust, opened the cover
And read so they all could hear.

When the purple sky is darkened
And the glow-worms do not shine,
When the air is cold and damp
And the trees grow out of time...
When the crystal streams stop flowing with life
And the flowers begin to sleep,
When their perfume fades
And their leaves drop off
And the daisies start to weep...

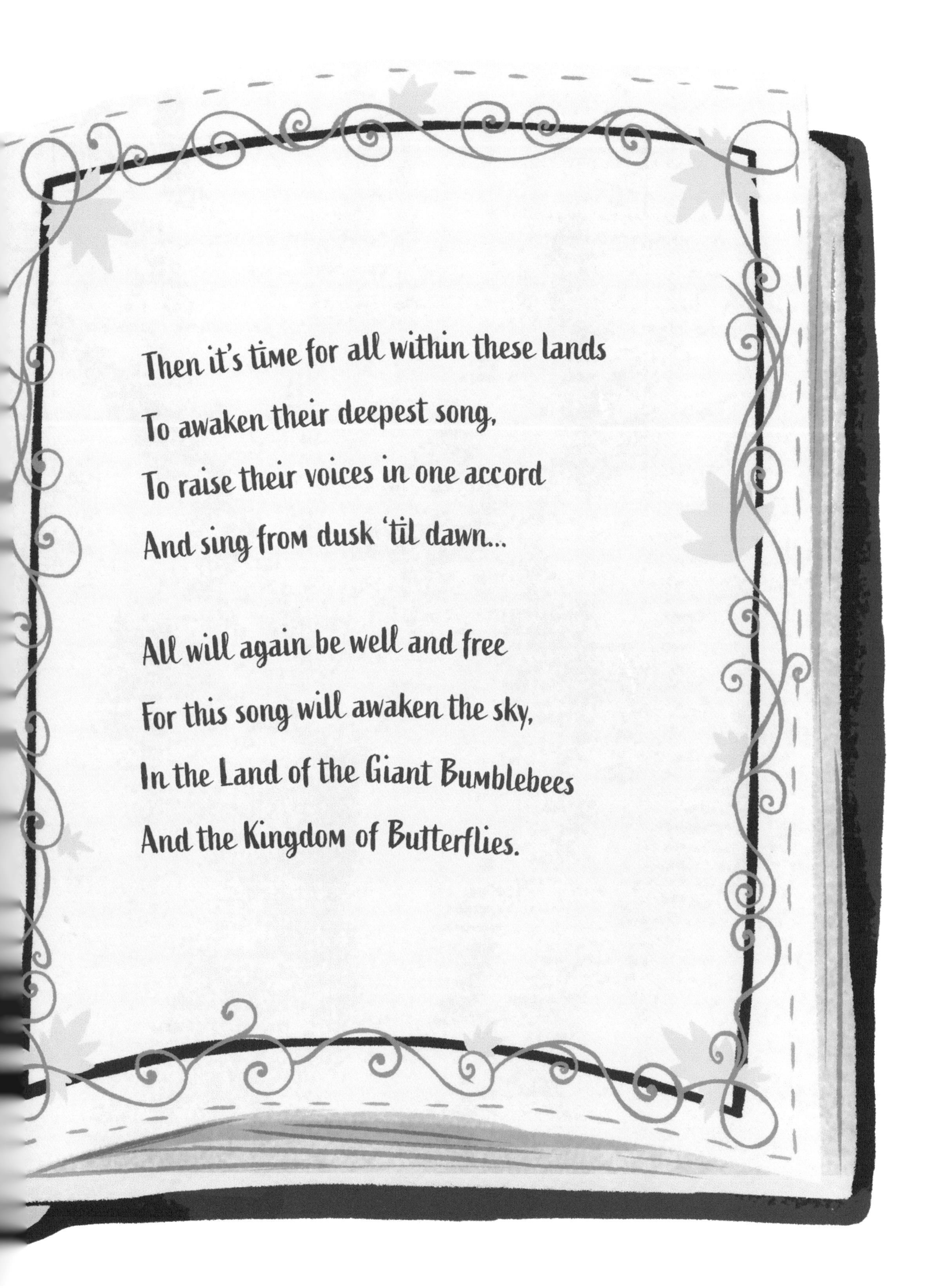
Then it's time for all within these lands
To awaken their deepest song,
To raise their voices in one accord
And sing from dusk 'til dawn...
All will again be well and free
For this song will awaken the sky,
In the Land of the Giant Bumblebees
And the Kingdom of Butterflies.

She closed the book with a mighty clap,
The butterfly king stood tall.
'It is time dear friends, to obey these words,
And sing–sing one–sing all!'

And throughout the land a chorus rose
It started soft and faint.
The melody danced on timid tongues
Yet grew steadily with each beat.

Until a mighty, glorious noise

Echoed like a waterfall.

Every creature was now singing

And their sound was quite joyful!

And the anthem sung with **hope** and **faith**
In the words of the sacred book,
Stirred life throughout the little land
In every glade and glen and brook.

The Queen smiled brightly at Lilia,
'Thank you!' she beamed and laughed.
'You have helped us restore our beautiful world;
You will always remain in our hearts.'

Then Buzz the giant bumblebee,
His wings began to flutter.
'Hop on little Lilia,' he said with a smile,

'It's time to go home to your mother.'

Lilia climbed up his hairy back,

Through the purple sky they

Up and down and around they soared

'Til the garden came back into view.

flew.

Slowly Lilia stepped out of the tree
And gave Buzz a parting hug.
'I hope I'll see you again my friend,
My favourite giant bug!'

With a hop,
a skip and a
jump she ran

Back to the house of her mother.
'I've had an amazing adventure!' she called,
'And I can't wait to have another!'

Then she told of the tree with the world inside
And how her words brought back to life,
The Land of the Giant Bumblebees
And the Kingdom of Butterflies.

The End